THE
ANZAC
BILLY

To my lovely Charlie. C.S.

To Albert James Patten (Grandfather), Gallipoli
John Jackson (Father), WWII
Michael (Brother), Vietnam. H.P. & M.J.

First published in Great Britain 2019 by Walker Books Ltd
87 Vauxhall Walk, London SE11 5HJ

2 4 6 8 10 9 7 5 3 1

Text © 2019 Claire Saxby
Illustrations © 2019 Mark Jackson and Heather Potter

This book has been typeset in Maiandra GD

Printed in China

British Library Cataloguing in Publication Data: a catalogue
record for this book is available from the British Library

ISBN 978-1-4063-8871-8

www.walker.co.uk

THE ANZAC BILLY

CLAIRE SAXBY · MARK JACKSON & HEATHER POTTER

WALKER BOOKS
AND SUBSIDIARIES
LONDON · BOSTON · SYDNEY · AUCKLAND

I'm filling a billy full of Christmas ...

for my dad.

On Monday, I put in my favourite butterscotch.

On Tuesday,
I put in his
favourite
yucky fish.

On Wednesday,
I put in the last
walnuts from
our tree.

On Thursday, I put in
a bar of chocolate.

On Friday, I put in
a just-knit pair of socks.

On Saturday, it was Mum's turn.

She added a razor
for his chin,
safety pins to
keep him in,
and soap to wash
his undies.

Dear Dad,

Though your Christmas
is in winter when it's
full summer here,
I'll close my eyes and make it
that we're sitting side by side.

Happy Christmas!

On Sunday,
Nanna filled the last spaces.
She squeezed in two
brand-new handkerchiefs,
and paper and a pencil
to write his letters home.

Dad's Anzac billy is just about full.

A billy can't be posted,
delivered on a bike,
or sent in a car,
truck or train.

It has to be loaded
on a ship with all those
other Anzac billies
for other soldier dads.

Nine billies to a layer,
three layers to a box.
Boxes stacked on boxes
to swing aboard the ship.

Won't they get mixed up?
How will they know
which one is his?
What if the ship is too slow?

Mum says I mustn't worry –
there's a Christmas billy
for every warfield soldier

filled by families, filled by friends.

Sail, big ship of billies,
sail far across the sea
until you reach the other side,
until you reach my dad.

I hope his billy makes it
and his Christmas Day is full
of songs to sing, some sunshine
and time to think of home.

If by chance this billy
reaches you and not my dad,
I hope you enjoy these treats, sir,
but please send my letter on.

Happy Christmas!